the songs of seven trees

55 new myths
for an old Wealden village

First published in 2015 by Mythbombing Publications

Visit www.mythbombing.com to find out more about the author and his work.

Typesetting thank yous:

With thanks to the The H.P.Lovecraft Historical Society
(http://www.cthulhulives.org/) for their unstinting diligence in reviving the
old fonts used in the time of Lovecraft, their 'HPLHS Oldstyle' font is used
throughout this work.

With thanks to the fonterly genius that is Jason Ramirez formally of
Pennyzine, now of Ground Control (http://thisisgroundcontrol.com/
wordpress/fonts/) for the use of 'Times New Omen' font.

With thanks and respect to Richard Kegler of the P22 Font Foundry (https://
www.p22.com/) for the use of the 'P22 Woodcut' font.

the songs of seven trees

55 new myths
for an old Wealden village
with illustrations by the author

Overheard, sought out, located, acquired, organized, compiled, catalogued, interpreted, maintained written-up, edited and illustrated, in the spirit of Ossian, Rowley, and Le Città Invisibili

by
Jonathan Mortimer

mythbombing
publications

Acknowledgements

With thanks to the people of the old Wealden village around which these fifty-five new myths have been spun.

Introduction

I have known the author of this curious collection of myths and fashioned folklore for far too many years, and consider myself lucky to have survived the experience with my head still relatively together. His world is rather different than mine, yet we live in the same corner of the country and work at the same sort of thing, he just sees it all from a different perspective, literally.

I often find him on the street, in the fields or besides the village pond, dressed in an unfortunate fisherman's smock, saggy hat askew, hands all filthy, scratching and scribbling away in his notebook. When I've asked him what he's about he's invariably said 'telling lies' with a shy smile. Well I'm no expert but his 'lies' seem to come about by sitting in the same place for hours, sometimes days, looking up at the scene ahead and back down to his lines as they build one upon the other, then back up again, as if he's in a life drawing class. He seems to pay a lot of attention to the world around him for someone who is making it all up. So perhaps the fabrication here is more akin to weaving tales out of the spaces between what is said, and around the things that didn't happen, very much like one of his stories in fact.

This I can attest to, every place depicted herein exists within a thrown stone of his front door, you would just have to put a bit of spin on it.

I've asked him what he does this for, what the goal is. and he's told me, in no uncertain words, that he wants these stories to 'stick', so place and tale become intertwined, landscape and myth as one. I've also asked him how long he thinks this might take, 'about a hundred years, I expect.' his smiling reply.

Alex Morgan

TREES OF THE VILLAGE

PLACES OF THE VILLAGE

PEOPLE OF THE VILLAGE

OBJECTS OF THE VILLAGE

ANIMALS OF THE VILLAGE

OUTSIDERS OF THE VILLAGE

TREES
OF THE VILLAGE

The myth of the Seven Trees

There is a village with **Seven trees** which stand in a tight ring. Tall trees, the tallest of all trees, giants from a very different land. These are old trees, belonging together, sisters of the same mind, they grow strong and true together.

1

Stand in the middle of these seven trees with your arms outstretched and you could almost brush each face of the trees soft bark with fingertip as you gently turn. Tight together these seven, roots intertwined and branches crossing, closer, tighter than they would grow without reason.

They stand togther but alone, in a field far from any other trees. A strange sight, but only momentarily, there is something very embracing about these seven, they want to hold you as they hold each other. There is power here, inside this ring, it calls some, and they come, and there can be a communion of sorts.

Those among the trees at the right time, that ask in the right way, may hear them sing their song, a song about the seven beginnings that were, and the seven endings that are to come, for some.

The myth of the Silver Tree

The children meet twice a year on Glebe Field for a day of games and challenges. The littlest ones run screaming and giggling along the road to the field, overly excited by months of preparation and speculation.

No one knows what the games will be as they change each time, therein lies the challenge, but there will be running and hiding and finding and dressing up and pretend and truth. The children will always end the day with the covering of the **Silver Tree**

It stands at the furthest corner of the field, branches glittering from the gilt that wraps every branch, twig and strip of bared bark. Back in the distant past, silver leaf was used to cover the tree, but now aluminium foil does the job just as well, carefully torn into pieces and burnished into place by the childrens' little fingers pushing the tissue thin metal into the dips and ridges.

From a distance this is an impressive sight and one the everyone here is very proud of, the sun strikes the tree and it appears to burst into flame and so the seasons are marked. Over the centuries the villagers have discovered that symbols work just as well as the old ways.

The myth of the Lying Tree

There is a **lying tree** in the
village. It is very small and rather easy to
ignore and it tells only a small untruth,
but lying trees are to be watched, one lie
can lead to others. The little lying tree
says it is a vine, it is not, it is an olive tree.

To the passer by the impression the tree
gives is a fair one, if you did not know
the difference you might be tricked by the
tree's gentle insistence. The lying tree
never fruits as that would break the lie,
and it bends and twists as a vine might
bend and twist, but anyone who looks and
thinks for a moment knows the duplicity.

Everyone knows it is a lying tree but
they do not confront it, they are not
cruel people and they understand that
the tree wants to be what it can never be.

After all it is the only lie it tells, in every
other way it is honest and true.

The myth of the Orchards

There are many **Orchards** around the village, apple orchards.

The blossom is a thing of wonder, and when it eventually falls the wind can take it and blow it around and through the houses like fragrant snowflakes. Those who know their Cats Head from their Pitmarston Pineapple will find every kind of apple represented.

4

There are thousands of different species of apple to be found with all kinds of rarities. The older trees, contorted from the centuries of birthing, can sometimes sprout new varieties on their branches, new fruits growing besides the old.

No one has ever surveyed the orchards with their many apples, no one has logged each variety, measured and recorded and counted from Adams Pearmain to the Zabergau Reinette. If an inventory was ever taken they would find the number creeping up with each passing season, new varieties created by agreement between the trees, new associations and mergers, consolidations and accords. The apple is a socially democratic tree.

The myth of the Roots

There are trees around the village that are much prized for their slow burning. You can often hear the chainsaws buzzing through the weekend as the people here prepare fuel for the winter. The trees are not an easy harvest however, their slow burning is due to their dense and heavy timber, it takes two strong men to lift a small section of branch and the trunk must be cut into small pieces to be carried into the truckbed or trailer. It can take a long and full day to cut down even the smallest of trees and each can fuel a home for many months.

The trees are easy to spot, their **roots** are exposed and the trunks are twisted and split. If you are out and about during the full moon you can hear the trees creak and moan under the tidal strain. The moon acts upon these trees, attracting the heavy timber up out of the ground, stretching and contorting their limbs.

The oldest trees have roots that sit, fully exposed upon the forest floor, each full moon they rise and drag across the open ground leaving scratch marks as they try to hang on to mother earth, occasionally one will lose and the moon will take a new prize captive.

The myth of the Tall Grasses

There is a man who lives in the village who plants seeds. On bright autumn mornings he walks the tall **grasses** t h a t border the southern   f i e l d s where the long neck sheep play. He carries a tall cane with which he pokes and scrabbles across the ground to loosen the soil before casting a handful of the tiny seeds, seeds he takes from his large poachers pockets.

These seeds grow to join the grasses, growing thick and deep, his grasses grow higher than the other plants, higher than the little apple trees, in time they grow higher than the houses.

But still, they are only grasses; they are fragile and have difficulty supporting their own weight. He tends the grasses, encouraging, filling in the gaps, replanting where necessary and joining up the growth to form corridors. If they are given the time and encouragement, these corridors will do what corridors do, lead to rooms. He plants them in lines stretching across the fields, and out across the county, and uses them to walk to all the other places that resonate and chime with the village.

6

The myth of the Disease Tree

This is a place of trees and grasses, flowers and fruit. The soil is rich and loamy a natural compost made up of thousands of years of vegetative growth, flourishing and then dying back, returning to the soil, death feeding the life that will inevitably take up that nutrient rich decay.

7

In the area of woodland that cups around the old vicarage stands the **disease tree**

This is a sacrificial tree that offers itself up to the canker and rot, the die-back and the leaf curl. It stands bleached and peeling, its bark shedding off, its branches exposed and bare. This is the antithesis of a Typhoid Mary, this is a willing, open limbed welcome that embraces each and every seasonal infection and malady, infestation and virus.

This tree forfeits its own well-being to preserve the vigour of the land that lies beneath the village, allowing the soil to retain the purity. The tree, in its ability and surrender to the wrongness that passes through the village goes further, it takes on each and every human trouble and woe, physical and mental, emotional and spiritual, it takes it all onto itself and suffers in courageous silence.

The myth of the Gathering

When the trees lose their leaves and needles they are gathered up with diligence and care. The young children meet up after school, baskets in hand, and skip through the little woods that pocket around the village, circling around every tree, swift sure fingers pinching up what the trees have dropped. Throughout the different seasons, after storm, wind and rain, for each of the different trees the gathering continues.

Nothing that was once living, is left to rot away. As winter approaches the children sew, weave and bind the leaves and needles, cones, pods and seeds, into blankets. When the first frost hits the winter festival is held, a weekend of celebration and preparation. The trees are decked in candles and the blankets are wrapped around each trunk, preparing them for the winter snows. This is a joyous and sacred act, it reaffirms the support and guidance that the trees bring, it remembers their heritage and their inheritance. The trees have the longest memories which they write into the pattern of their growth. Maintaining the trees is the best way of preserving those stories, even though no human can ever read them.

PLACES
OF THE VILLAGE

The myth of the Turn

In the centre of the village, besides the church and its venerated dead the road **turns** tightly on itself, forcing the vehicles passing through to crawl tentatively, ready to brake, and backing up uncomfortably around the bend when another vehicle is coming on unseen.

This a favoured spot for the residents to sit of an evening and watch the unfamiliar negotiate the unknown, smiling as the shiny metal scrapes against shiny metal, high tech impact absorbing rubber, steel and aluminium brushing old stone and traditional brick and losing. Drivers squatting to assess damage and consider costs, exchange details or debate blame. No driver is ever really to blame, the village is responsible, it flexes and stretches the bend to ensure the difficulty remains, no matter how often an outsider takes the turn the experience is a fresh one.

The table in the window bay of the pub is most prized as it has a raised position that affords a particularly good view down on the road and you will rarely find a seat free there during summer or winter alike. Every one likes a little outsider strife over their beer.

The myth of Antiques

One of the few shops in the village is the **antiques** shop.

You will know it by the little collection of furniture that is displayed outside, the many drawered writing desk and children's sized straight back chair, the bookcase and the painted plates. Step inside and the tiny interior opens up to a compressed complexity of potential wonders.

There can be no other interior that holds so many intricate delights, boxes within chests beneath tables stacked with books their pages heavy with pressed plants and letters home. There are things that were once beautiful and things once loved, things once important, things once irrelevant, but now they sit patiently, expectantly, waiting for their second life, which may never come. For all its charm there is nothing here that is necessary, nothing needed, nothing you would not be better off without.

A person can spend an hour or a day or an eternity inside the little shop, going deeper while standing still, but the owner is a kindly man who will usher you out if he feels that you are reaching too far beyond your time and place.

10

The myth of the Ships

The older villagers sometimes tell tales of a sea that once surrounded the village. **Ships** of shallow draft and heavy oak beam were constructed from spliced branch and split trunk, they say, ships that went looking for wind and fortune. There are three shallow indents in a field which point to such industry. The surrounding low lying terrain is flat, the soil sandy with tiny shells and with eyes closed you can feel something immense may once have crept up to this place.

11

There are villages and towns further south which can point to their shipbuilding heritage, telling of Henry's decree and patronage, of Edward, Edmund and Alfred, of brave craft built in a time of war and sent out to carry the good name of the people that fashioned it.

But the sea, when it lapped around the village, was an ancient sea, before the word came to these islands, when the sun was a goddess and the rhythm of the seasons was controlled with song and offerings. The villagers have a long memory, they cannot forget because to do so would be to lose something of themselves, of who they were and, they believe, may be again, and the sound of the sea is insistent in their ears if long vanished from their eyes.

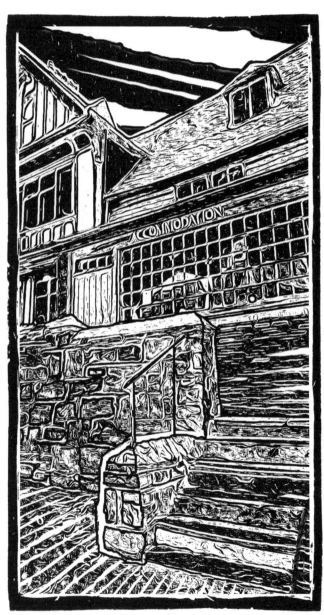

The myth of the Pub

The village **pub** sits besides the church and does everything it can with its timber and painted plaster face to distance itself from the stoic honey stone of the church tower.

The pub has a name on its swinging sign but it is not the one it knows itself by, it has an older name, before the car park, the international menu and the imported beer.

The pub wears a different face to go with its different name, look back through photographs of the high street and you will see the pub looking more modern the further back that the photograph is taken.

This is not a question of developing patina, not a question of the tricks of shadow and eye, the facade of the pub has aged not in its weathering but in its origination. Today you would call it tudor in style, the timber beams are dark with memory, brick floors groove worn from generations of patrons, but in photographs taken a hundred years ago it has a georgian face, built of crisp regular brick and neatly painted panel windows.

It would be interesting to stand here in front of this curious building a hundred years into the future, and see what this backwards aging building has become, perhaps post and wattle, earthern walls and thatch. If we could travel backwards in time, three, five hundred years, a millennium, the architectural style of the building would become more modern, you would see glass and steel, composite acrylics and tensile fabrics.

Go back further still and you would see something sitting here on this place that would make you question your eyes, trust them and there would be all the answers that you could wish for, to any question that you could imagine.

The myth of the Passages

Behind the little main street are parallel smaller roads, barely more than paved tracks, single cars only, access and deliveries, you know the sort of thing.

Beyond these secondary roads lie tracks, footpaths and bridleways, trotting horses and couples walking hand in hand.

Beyond these are the paths, worn into the grass, and past these are the memories, invisible but no less apparent.

Each of these byways is linked by passages From the main street the passages slink off between the buildings, hidden among ribbed details and folded shadows, only recognised when one stands directly in front of them.

The passages that link the next are more discrete, glimpsed only in reflection. The passages past these are felt with fingertips not seen, and beyond these the passages are not for the corporeal but the spirit.

You may see a villager walking down the street and then as you are distracted, dissappear, looking-glass in hand, they have business on the outer paths.

The myth of the Road

There is a **road** north of the village called Seven Mile Lane. This is a road now, busy with traffic going somewhere, but it was once just a little lane, little more than a track, and it was once seven miles in length, but now it is more, this road grows.

Many years ago Seven Mile Lane had one tip on the outskirts of the village, it afforded the villagers a convenient, straight passage to the market of the nearest, biggest, town where business could be carried out and exchanges made. This was a village road and it followed village ways, the road knew its place, knew its role and did what it could to do it well.

On market days the road would contract, reducing the distance just a little, not enough to stress the surrounding countryside, just a little tightening of the spaces between the physical elements and materials that made the reality solid.

After the market day the road would relax back to its full length, imperceptibly releasing the tension and creaking back to seven miles. This rhythm of stretch and release became habitual, became what it did, what it was.

Over time the market moved, as businesses are want to, but the road kept to the rhythm, the town in which the market stood shrank in importance and eventually town, market and meaning disappeared from the map and the memory.

But the road kept reaching out to a place now long gone, it felt along the texture of the ground like a blind man in a strange land tip tapping along unfamiliar edges. Each week, each year stretching out in expectation of catching hold of the fringe of the lost village.

The road is now lost in its sightless struggle to find its purpose, like some massive undersea creature venturing out across the abysmal deep it has torn away from its root and is alone in the blackness. Seven Mile Lane is many miles north of the village now, the villagers no longer see it as one of their own, it is a lost traveller.

The myth of the Hallowed

Once a year the villagers leave their homes at midnight, candles in hand, and walk slowly and in procession to the graveyard.

This **hallowed** day is one that the villagers treat with full solemnity, the days that precede it are ones of preparation, the graveyard grass is trimmed, the vases filled with flowers, the villagers cleanse mind body and the clothes that they wear. The days that follow it are of reflection.

There they stand on the circle brick path laid around the gravestones, enclosing and encompassing, and they wait out the night. Some hold hands; others form loose knots of association and relation formed of history and liability, but most stand silent and alone, their thoughts elsewhere.

As the sun breaks the darks' hold the villagers turn and walk slowly home again. Throughout the night no one speaks, no prayers are given or rituals played out, this is a responsibility, to watch over those lost, those given over, those offered and those taken, on this, their one night of weakness.

The myth of the Story Lines

Around the village there are **story lines**
These are not paths defined by gravel and
gate, just well worn lines that cross fields
and gardens, grass abraded to soil, stone
polished to a smooth gloss, tarmac taken
down to the stone chip bed. The story
lines are thin, made by one foot being
placed carefully in front of the other.

The lines loop across fields and gardens,
over fences and walls, ditches and streams,
they turn back on themselves, run alongside
other lines and sometimes seem to question
where they are going, turning back on
themselves, wandering into corners and out
again, wiggling and wobbling as if indecisive.

The lines never reach a destination, the lines
never come to an end, the lines never stop, they
weave. If you float high over the village and
the sun catches the lines just right, perhaps
you will see the image that they make, the
drawing that they trace out across the land.

One day a year the villagers walk the lines,
careful to precisely place each foot, keeping
the line as narrow and defined as they can.
In walking the lines the story comes to life a
little in their minds, and they remember.

16

The myth of the Tower

Mobile phone reception here is intermittent and prone to harsh crackle, crossed signals and sudden terminations. This might be a surprise to those who have travelled through the village, as on its eastern outskirts is what looks to all like a mobile phone tower

17

This is a false impression as the tower is not part of any national telecoms network; it receives and broadcasts a very different signal. The tower is managed and maintained by Martin, a dedicated father of two who serves the village well. He gives tours of the facility to younger villagers as part of their education in to the deeper workings of the community, even showing the braver ones down to the fourth basement from which the Pit itself can be seen.

Twice a year the two mile stretch of road that leads out of the village and past the tower, is closed. The overnight closure is marked by flashing warning lights and diversion signs, orderly and planned, lasting from dusk until dawn. This allows for the transportation to take place unseen by those who would be better off unknowing.

The myth of the Lines

There used to be a railway in the village, in a time of steam and coal, but it has been closed for so long that no one is quite sure where it was. The track has gone also but if you walk west you will feel it in your boots, a memory of vibration, of the ground shimmering under the weight of the locomotive as it chuffed and bullied its carriages up the hill.

18

The railway lines are both powerful symbols and a physical imposition upon the land, metal rails acting as continuous conduits for the energy of the train, and any other energy that wants a free ride on a willing conductor. Tracks are a kind of artificial ley line and once established these lines persist, iron is a powerful metal, it retains a memory of land and contains an echo of its lost love, although the iron is long gone, the memory and love remain.

The trees that line these memories respond to these strings of power, they cup and contain it in channels of growth that mirror the brick tunnels of 'ago'.

You can feel the potentiality here as a chilled patient calm.

The myth of the Hill

The village sits atop a little **hill** that rises out of flat ground. The hill is steep if you walk it, gentler to the north and the rolling landscape that billows out from the hill, but abrupt to each of the other compass points, of which there are five in this corner of the country although no one but the locals know this. The hill is green, the buildings being careful not to slide too far off the crest, pressing together like people bunched together on a melting block of ice in a warm sea.

The villagers believe that on a clear day and with sharp enough eyes, you can see far enough back in time to understand just about anything you have a mind to, and when the wind is right you can hear your own first cries.

You'll see them perched in the hill, picnicing on blankets with wicker baskets stuffed with pickles and preserves, but silent, no one speaking because they come here to listen, and to remember.

On special days the villagers call on Robin Goodfellow to allow them to look forward through their lives and if they are unlucky they get their wish.

19

The myth of the Ruin

There is a picturesque **ruin** outside the
village, of an abbey once grand and important,
too much so, thought the King, so he had the
place burned and many of the monks with it.
The stones stand now without roofs to support
or parishioners to encompass, marking the
nave and chapel with grass and wild flowers.

The villagers picnic here on the weekends
when the sun is warm, they take their baskets
of bread and cheese and bottles of local
wine and they sit on the same spots where
the pious gave their lives for their beliefs.

Each of these spots is eagerly sought after
and they jostle and bicker like starlings
on a branch until they are established for
the day and the merriment can begin.

They revel not in the place but in its demise,
they raise their plastic glasses and chink their
pastries in celebration of destruction, not in
death, not in support of a King or his rule,
not in the persecution or the possessions lost,
not in the land riven or the people driven out.
The toast that rings out is for fire and stone,
the burning of the very stuff of the planet
on which they now stand and which they one
day hope to leave behind.

The myth of the Pond

Villages across the region have a comparable set of features and highlights, the church, the common field, the handful of shops around the memorial, and the pond

If we could travel far enough away we could look back we would see this pond performing its duty of the centuries, the people meeting to wash their clothes, beating the cotton against the stone surrounds, the stocks of fresh water fish netted for celebration days, the cattle kneeling to drink from the edge.

The pond has a feature that points to its earliest use. There is a fence that surrounds the pond on all sides, and around that fence is another fence that acts to reaffirm the duty of its partner. These two rings of restriction prevent the casual and the foolhardy, the honest mistake and the wanton ignorance.

The pond is black and deep, so deep that any coin thrown will drift slowly for the lifetime of the person that has thrown it, never resting, always further to fall. Any person foolish enough to swim in the pond will be drawn down into its eternal nothingness, an absence of feeling and light. There can be no end while the village stands.

The myth of the Graves

In the middle of the village, at the highest point, is the church, warm stone capped in clay tile. Around the church are the graves of the villagers who have lived here and passed on but will never leave.

22

The graveyard is small and the people many, and so the graves are built one upon the other and the ground slowly thickens and swells.

There is no history that dates the origins of the village, but if you were to age it by its layered dead, like the rings on a tree, you would count back into times outside that which history can describe. There is a heavy stone wall that has been built around the graveyard to contain the growing ground. The level of the grass is now above the head of most, and the wall is reinforced and in places straining to hold back its population.

There are more dead than living, and the dead have the best of views in their multi-storey resting places. But the waistband is straining and every villager knows that there must be a limit, they do their very best to avoid adding themselves to the problem.

OBJECTS OF THE VILLAGE

The myth of Gates

There are three small wooden gates
that always remain locked although no one
has a key. These gates are not very high and
the areas beyond them are easily accessible
by other routes, come across a latched and
locked gate and you can simply walk the long
way around to get where you want to go.

23

The villagers ignore the gates; they see them
as the walls they sit within, natural borders
and barriers dividing garden, road and field.

The gates themselves are not so old and
not so special to warrant special interest,
the tourists who pull over in their cars
to photograph the scenic vistas and the
picturesque brick and tile pass them by. But
they are as close to an answer as any of us
could ever find. If, as a visitor, you were
to see one of these little gates ajar it would
be better if you didn't venture through,
better by far to go the long way round.

These gates lead to places beyond that which
is visible, beyond that which can tolerate the
corporeal.

The myth of the Sleepers

When the railway was torn up by the outsiders the villagers found use for much of the flesh and bones that were left behind. The concrete **sleepers** which had replaced the old timber ones only a few years previously, were left in place when the rails were removed so the villagers picked up each one, one after the other, and carried them up to the village.

The sleepers were reused throughout the village, some you will find in gardens, as lintels and raised beds, some you will find supporting cellars and propping up retaining walls, some went to the Pit to shore up the mine. Most though you'll find on the pathways that snake out and around the village, giving a little more grip on the muddy slopes, and these paths can get very slippery when the festivals and parades are into their third days and the lines of villagers have circled the hill and sung their songs.

24

The myth of Wires

Walk through the village looking up and you see **wires** strung across road and p a t h , **wires** trailing gable and hip, wires tight, wires sagging low, wires cresting in waves, dipping in troughs, wires slipping into houses through lifted tile and beneath window sills like diving swallows.

The wires run from telegraph poles to each of the houses, just like in many a place, but these are not telephone lines, these lines carry no words and wishes, these are lines of demarcation and linkage.

House to house the line is strung, tying the people through physical twine, ensuring that relationships are maintained, this is a place of connections, but connections that exist high over the streets, not within the homes themselves, the lines mean that you do not have to speak with your neighbour, the lines connect what needs connecting, freeing the people here to maintain a distance and insularity when they venture out on the street.

The myth of the Sign

There is a **sign** besides the little pond in the centre of the village. The sign indicates the four choices the traveller has at the crossroads, to each of the nearest neighbouring hamlets and towns that occupy the compass points.

Take a closer look and you will see that the names of the places on each of the four arms of the sign are in different styles of letter. It is only something that the over observant would register but it is there and every now and then a visitor is seen walking around the sign looking up at it. Those few probably conclude that the different arms are from different times and the fashion for clarity has changed over the decades.

If these same observers were to return to the sign a few days later they would see that thesign has changed once again, that the black paint has refashioned itself into new styles of letter and layouts of word. A gentle and endless transformation that rolls across the timber as the roads roll off towards other places with other signs.

The myth of the Woodpile

The chimneys of the houses in the here are tall and wide, square and strong. Beneath each chimney the Janus fireplaces, big enough to stand in, big enough to lie down in, face into each neighbouring house. The fireplaces are well used, warming homes and workplaces with oak and elm that crackles quietly as it is consumed. Each house has a stack of timber drying in the garden, each woodpile is arranged in a loose triangle, each facing East.

27

If you were to remove the roofs of the houses and peer down you would see that the fireplaces are built as needed demand within the homes but only the woodpiles are consistent and fixed in their position, they are the most considered and rigorously aligned part of each and every house.

This is because that although fire is important, the potential for fire is more so, the wood in the piles is waiting for the fire and preparing itself and is therefore given the respect of the willing sacrifice.

The myth of the Roofs

The **roofs** of the village are intricate and complex. All the houses in the village have roofs which are longer at the back than at the front. If you walk up the main street you see houses like many another, but perhaps you would notice that the roofs seem a little more convoluted than you might expect. If you were invited behind the facade you might see these same roofs dipping low to the ground, you having to bend to tuck your head under their beams and gutters.

28

This asymmetrical aspect is part of the rhythm of the village, and part of its strength, the roofs are built to take the majority of the rainfall away from the centre of the village.

The little high street is a few drops drier than the green fields and meadows that surround the village. This difference is important as it helps in the conducting of the ground electricity that forms the ring that protects, prevents and empowers.

This village is a large but simple machine with a complex operation.

The myth of Streetlights

There are no **streetlights**
in the village, not in the road, not around
the pond, not lighting up the church. At
night it is dark, dark enough to make you
see what cannot be there. The darkness is a
physical thing, you can feel it between thumb
and finger, it has a texture and a weight.

29

If you walk a little way down the lane of the
blind you will see the last streetlight that lit
the unforgiving ground here. It is a
pretty thing with mosaic mirror set in a
butterfly winged cowl over a single lamp.
Quite beautiful and quite singular, it
exists as one of the crossovers from
another version of this village, stranded
and alone and quite literally out of place.

This lamp has no power, the lamp is
cold, but if you could bring your own
energy to it you might use it to do
wonderful things, go wonderful places.

If you strain up, tip toe, looking closely at
the mirrors you'll see a reflection of yourself,
but a very different you standing in a very
different place.

The myth of Fog

There is a small stream that runs through the valley that defines the villages western edge. Although small it runs fast and eager, when it gets the encouragement it likes to flood out across the fields that border it, creating new lakes where crops and cattle stood the day previous.

30

When the stream floods and the air is willing there can be a **fog** that rolls up and around the village like the sea lapping at the little hillock.

Once in a long while this sea tide builds up and overflows in to the village itself, creeping with curious exploratory delicacy through the streets and around the houses. Sometimes the fog is so dense that you cannot see nor hear, every sense is blocked by total absence.

Everyone stays at home when the fog comes, too many things do not look the way they should, the fog takes something away from the reality of the place.

Fog should conceal, should hide, but here in hiding it reveals.

The myth of Wine

The **wine** that they make in the village, from the sloping fields that fringe the hill, is uncomplicated and a little bitter, it can taste salty as if used to sea breezes.

31

The vines are old and twisted, contorted about themselves and the grapes are wrinkled, weathered and often withered and small. The vines are untended and wild with the villagers only visiting them at the harvest. The grapes have a kind of ignoble rot which the villagers believe give them their special flavour, one that reminds them of times past.

The wine tends to be dark, opaque, so that if one holds it up to the sun the light loses its way in the completeness of it. It suits the villagers very well this wine and they drink it with abandon. The wine stains the teeth of the older villagers, it gives them the look of someone who bites their tongue and worries the little gashes so that they refuse to heal.

It stains the heart too, this wine, but that is harder to see.

PEOPLE
OF THE VILLAGE

The myth of the Weaver

There is a man in the village who **weaves**
There have been weavers here since the
Dutch brought their delicately industrial
ways to the area hundreds of years ago, but
this man does not weave cloth. He sits by the
high window of his tall house, high up in the
steeply pitched roof, it is a projecting bay
designed to capture every moment of sunlight.

32

He has a loom, of sorts, and thread that
he winds and stretches through holes and
around pegs with delicate precision because
he is weaving dreams. The loom is an
heirloom, handed down, but he repairs,
replaces and enhances every time he sits
down at it. It is a living thing this loom,
with mood swings and outbursts, but he
knows it better than he knows himself, he
knows when to stay quiet and when to weave.

He weaves during the day when the light is
good and the street is busy with life being
lived. If you stand outside his house you can
just hear the swish of the thread as he makes
it dance around and through its partners.
forgotten things from ignored places.

The weaver spends his nights walking
slowly through the streets here, pausing

by window and door to hear the murmurs and sighs of his days work.

He takes little forgotten things from ignored places, fragments of lives lived and hopes harboured and collects them in his heavy coat with its many deep pockets, like a poacher taking slumbering game from its perch and den. At his loom he pulls out the little memories he has collected, a piece of twig, a strand of hair and torn corner of a discarded letter, and he weaves them into his understanding of the people and the place, the time gone and the time to come.

All these pieces are tied through his careful administration into such complex interconnecting possibilities as to bind the people into a single garment that the village itself then wears. Or so he believes, it is possible that he is dreaming it.

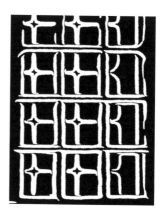

The myth of the Speaker

On Sunday mornings there is an opportunity for anyone in the village to speak freely and openly to all. Beside the pond in the middle of the village, under the village sign, a stepped dais, small and sturdy, allows the speaker a proper sense of the moment.

33

Not everyone takes their turn and it does not happen every week but everyone knows that the opportunity will come and that they have a right to be heard, and this does much to smooth any ripples or possible conflicts. At birth each villager is given their twelve Speaking Days which range across the expected life of each member depending on the trade they will pursue, the role they are expected to play. These twelve opportunities are part of the sacrament, they cannot be taken away.

Outsiders are not encouraged but not prevented, if you listen to a villager speak you will hear them thank the village, the people and the place, the water and the soil. If you listen between the words you may occasionally hear something that might sound like doubt.

The myth of the Jogger

At night the **jogger** runs. When everyone and everything is asleep, he thumps with heavy strides through the village, around and around the same regular route.

This is unknown to all, no one is there to question what this running is for, why this jogger runs the same way each night, never pausing, face grim, determined and with a job to finish.

34

No one is there to time, if they were they would register surprisingly consistent laps, rain or cold the route around the village takes exactly the same time for this running man. But then it isn't a question of improvement for this villager, this is their punishment and their reward, for a misdeed not committed but dreamed.

The punishment befits the crime and therefore takes place in the scene of the transgression, each and every night until the penance is done. This is a self administered punishment, and the jogger cannot forgive himself and so the parole is put back each time it approaches and the night running carries on.

The myth of the Hunts

The village makes money from **hunts** its which it stages with all the trappings of long held tradition. The clothes worn on hunting days are specific to the animal sought, it is a mark of respect to dress appropriately, trousers pressed and sharp edged, shirts white beneath tight waistcoats.

35

The bags that the hunters bring the game home in are made in the village itself, waxed cotton and leather, bees and calf grown and harvested for the purpose. Each is sewn by hand, each the same but with an important difference. The bag makers prick their fingers as they turn back the seams, dropping a little blood on the fabric before sealing it behind stitched wax walls.

Each hunter is given a bag, at the end of the day each bag is heavy with feather and fur. Of course the hunters, down from the big city for the day, think that they are shooting pheasant, deer, and rabbit; the warming drinks handed out at the start of the day ensure that they only see what they expect to see.

The myth of Washing

There are no **washing** machines in the village, well, very few, the pub has some rooms it lets out so they have a machine for convenience sake. Most of the village, certainly all of the ordinary residents, have no washing machines and no drying machines. These are considered too loud, too disruptive, too much part of the outside world.

The villagers are clean enough though, no one misses the mechanical help. The villagers hang their dirty washing on their clothes lines and wait for the rain to rinse through and the sun to dry and freshen. It is a satisfactory method which everyone agrees is far more appropriate than the alternatives.

You will always see clothes fluttering in the wind, clean clothes drying and dirty clothes waiting for rain.

36

The myth of Eyes

The villagers are a diverse group, at least to look at. They are tall and short and portly and lithe, varied and assorted. Their faces look like any face you would see anywhere, every variety of characteristic, scale and hue.

37

The villagers are representative, but not of the area around them which is rather more singular in its genus, instead the villagers' spread of facial characteristics harks back to a earlier time, before Toba and the great dark that followed it.

Where the people here do relate is in their

Everyone has green eyes. Sometimes their eyes might look green-grey or green-brown, green-gold or green-blue and you might put that down to the sunlight and shadow, or the reflections of surroundings, but truthfully the eyes are windows onto their emotions and any impression of colour are due to how they are feeling at that particular moment.

At night their eyes look black.

The myth of the Longest Day

On the **longest day**
the chosen will gather at sunrise and re-enact the war between winter and summer, two seasons that never meet yet squabble for dominance over the land.

38

With sticks and cries they club the sun and its keepers through the time honoured ritual of combative dance, legs banded in metal spikes, feet shod in steel heavy leather and iron studs. Each wears the clothes handed down, badges and ribbons of honour and hats hand woven from the grasses found in the fields around the village.

To the rhythm of song and chant they dance towards and away, sticks flashing down on the head and shoulders of their partner, if their own stick is not brought up in time to parry and strike their own blow. It has been this way for a thousand years, this symbolic warring that negates the need for the seasons to meet in conflict and has guaranteed the smooth passage of the seasons through all that time.

This is a civilised kind of sacrifice, there is blood but there is rarely a loss of life. The following day the sun always rises.

The myth of Birthday Cards

There is a lady in the village who writes
birthday cards

She is an elderly woman now, moving with more care than she did just a couple of years previously, and she's been the village card writer since she was a teenager. She writes them every day, every morning and evening, her afternoons are her own.

She's writes them seven days a week, and never goes on holiday, the job of the card writing is too important to let slip. She does not count them and there is no quota, but to anyone who watches her as she diligently posts each individual envelope into the red box in the middle of the village they would guess at one hundred a day, thousands every month.

One might wonder how she knows so many people, and if you were to ask her she would smile sweetly, and answer another question entirely. She writes cards to people she does not know, young and old, rich and poor, near and impossibly far. She writes the names on the card and the addresses on the envelope, and she does not know where either comes from, they just occur to her.

The myth of the Keeper

There is a village with seven trees and in that village there is a shop. This is the village shop, it serves this little community selling the ordinary and the everyday, the food, supplies, goods, bads, taking care of the little things that you need in your day to day.

Everything that the shop sells it sells in packets and boxes and tins. Nothing in the shop is allowed to come out of its wrapper, everything for sale must wear the discretion of plastic or paper or metal. The aisles are packed tightly with these packaged goods, seemingly randomly spread upon the shelves. Standing back we see a rhythm to the placement, the goods are arranged by the colour of the box within which they are sold. The lights are bright, hurting the eyes, nothing is to be in shadow, nothing but colour and vibrancy.

The shop **keeper** wears black, black and grey, but under his bright blue lightweight nylon warehouse coat, a coat he keeps tightly buttoned. He sits on his wooden stool concealing his desire for the muted and the quiet as he watches over the rows of brashly coloured and orderly coordinated packaging. A secret rebel.

The myth of the Souls

There are eight hundred and twenty **Souls** living in the village, so says the records that tell of this place, that try to measure and box up the immeasurable, unboxable. Eight hundred and twenty, and there always has been, since the first measuring back when Kings wore dull swords, when Lords scrapped themselves clean with sharpened bone and Elders delivered their justice with club and lance. Eight hundred and twenty, since the moon and sun fought the sky for the role of God and the wild beasts were first corralled into docile larders.

Eight hundred and twenty, and there always will be. When a baby is born someone moves on, makes way, so that the balance is maintained. You would have to go back to the very beginning, before the ice, to find the one, the first, after whom everything else became.

It is this original villager that is shown carved in stone and built into the brickwork, scratched in wood and cast in the clay of the tiles. Each house has a likeness of the first, it is a mark of respect and ownership.

The myth of Mushrooms

There is a cafe in the village that offers a traditional breakfast of eggs and toast, much loved by the early morning crowd, the labourer and the insomniac. They serve the kinds of simple cooked breakfast you can get far and wide in this country of early risers and early fallers.

42

With every meal you get mushrooms whether you ask for them or not, whether you like them or not. This is the cafe's way and everyone is understanding of its particularities, nearly everyone. Sometimes, if a customer does not understand the rules the mushroom must be secreted beneath a crispy piece of toast or chopped up fine in the eggs.

Sometimes the mushrooms are rubbed across the surface of the cooked ham, or a little of the broth of the stewed mushrooms added to the coffee, if coffee is all you have ordered. But you always have mushrooms. you must always have mushrooms with your dish. They grow the mushrooms themselves, in the basement, the floor deep in forest litter. Keeping the quality high and the nutrients in balance, because only the cafe knows just how important these funghi are to the emotional well-being of the village.

The myth of Digging

106

This is a village of gardeners. At the weekend you see them pruning, sweeping, mowing and **digging**

This, it seems, is not a hobby but perhaps more of a responsibility. You won't find the villagers whistling as they work, and it is perfectly possible to see neighbours gardening away on either side of their fences without a word spoken, this then is more duty than pleasure, more chore than leisure.

43

The gardens of the village are pretty enough, you see the roses, lupins and sweetpea as you would find in any of the surrounding villages.

If you could just sit and watch them over the course of an afternoon in the garden, busying away with barrows, trowels and trays of seedlings you might think that perhaps there's rather more digging than is strictly necessary and that the villagers rarely seem to add compost to their borders and beds.

Indeed they seem to be mixing, moving and even removing soil, one might suspect that they were looking for something down there.

The myth of the Game

Like many of the villages in this part of the country there is a tradition of invented or adapted **games** that the locals play with each other to the mild confusion of anyone casually observing the proceedings. Most are card games with convoluted rules or checkers type games played with beads or coins, loser buying the drinks.

In the village the game most often seen played is a little more complicated, but it can be played on any flat surface between two villagers of any age and with any number of playing pieces. You see it in the pub and cafe but if you want to guarantee a game then the picnic table besides the pond has a seemingly continuous game being played with different players stepping in and out regularly throughout the day but the pieces staying in play.

Any outsiders glancing at a couple of villagers in game might not immediately register the reality of active competition, it taking perhaps the murmured approval of an onlooker appreciating a particular move or the groan of a player as an unforeseen move is made against them to announce it's presence.

Once made aware of the competitive silence

44

between the players, an observer might still confuse an ongoing game as nothing more than a curious intensity between the two sitters as there are no recognised playing pieces in the game, instead any object on the table can be press-ganged into service as active piece, backed up by trinkets and oddments brought out from a players pocket.

A game often revolves around little more than the considered placement of sugar bowl, salt seller and cutlery, with each player seemingly having control of every piece, following some byzantine ruling of rights and obligations, like a free moving game of chess without marked board or designated pieces, without the limitations of pieces limited in movement or the need to conquer another's Queen to win.

It is as if the table pieces are only the physical representation of a game played in the mind, the cup and the napkin being the tip of some conceptual challenge that is poking through into reality from somewhere outside.

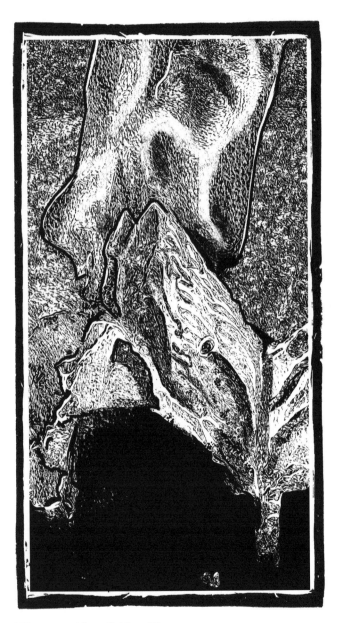

The myth of the Burn

The sun blesses the village more than is strictly fair. Although it would be more honest to say that the clouds shy away from the village. The villagers take turns to ensure that it stays this way, meeting on the little hill overlooking the village to say the words that have been said since the beginning and pay a little penance.

45

The villages enjoy their sunlit winter days and their warm summers. Like many people the villagers like to cook outside, with open fires, smokeries, barbecues all active throughout the year. The fires are lit early in the morning and maintained through the day into the evening, the people gather, bringing their own meat to the grille.

Even on the days when the cloud cannot be held back the villagers know that it is always sunny above the clouds and they light their fires anyway. They remember when the ground had less attraction for them than it does now, when the sun powered their lives.

The villagers sit in their gardens and **burn** their flesh, on their backs and on their grilles. The smoke curls up and, high above them it merges into wispy clouds that smell of meat.

The myth of the Children

The **children** of the village are like many others, and are encouraged to be so. They dress in the fashion of the moment; they head off to school with superhero lunch box and sports bags, they laugh and talk in idioms and clipped narratives, slipping mercurially from one subject to the next and back around, only their own being able to keep apace.

There is nothing Midwich about these children, nothing of the other, they are happy, healthy and full of the potential filling every youngster in every far-flung land.

Perhaps the children of the village express their potential in slightly more complex ways than their outer cousins, the blend a little more composite, more elaborate, and their pathways more defined.

Look in the eyes of so many children in this world and you'll see a relaxed confidence; in the village it is the same, the only difference being that the children here know what they have confidence in.

46

ANIMALS OF THE VILLAGE

The myth of the Seer Horses

In the lower field live the three

seer horses

Each has a mask, made of rough sackcloth, wrapped to cover from nose to mane, with pointed ears and binding straps to keep the cotton tight.

47

The masks keep the summer flies away and the winter thoughts in. The horses see much from within their sacks, although if you peer through the rips and tears in the masks you will see that their eyes are closed. This would surprise the uninitiated but then they would not know that these three horses know more about the future than is healthy, these are seer beasts which can be called upon to foretell and forestall and the villagers fear them.

They have lived in their field since the before times and have foreseen much that has come to pass and much that has yet to come, but will.

The villagers never ask the seer horses to reveal their knowings, they are left alone in their field, given offerings of fruit and fresh hay and each have a new cotton mask sewn to them each year.

The myth of Cats

They have many **cats** in the village.

No household owns a cat but every house has a cat, although sometimes shared with many neighbours. At different points of the year some houses have two cats, some have three, dependant on where the sun warms the sofa, or the chicken graces the bowl.

48

The cats are family, they share a common line, an ancestor, each is a little wild, a little independent, but they blink in respectful acknowledgement when they cross paths with a fellow. With the humans they pass by, looking the other way, intent on feline things. But the cats can be found spread full length in front of the fireplaces in the evening.

The villagers welcome the cats, greeting them with soft words and blankets, sharing heat and meat. But these are distant cats, you will not find them on a lap or twining around your legs with affectionate calls. These are cats that know your place.

There are no dogs in the village, at least none as pets, the only dogs are required to work for their keep. The cats are never asked to do anything but look beautifully malign.

The myth of the Night Horse

The **night horse** is white and brown and curious. It bobs casually down the little lane barely registering the verbal encouragements and kicky snappy commands of the woman sitting on his back. She owns this horse, proudly so, but he doesn't see it that way, doesn't understand possession. He struggles enough with his perception of self, his place in the world to worry about her as well.

When he is alone in his box he often wonders whether he 'is', and if he is then what is the purpose of this 'being', what is everything aiming towards, what is the end point, how will anyone know when they have finished and they can all just stop. He wonders about the 'me' inside himself. He rubs his face against the wall of his stall to feel his own shape, to deduce the envelope that the 'me' sits within.

It's worse at night when the darkness within him leaks out and fills the world. Everywhere around is shrouded in his lack of belief, his non-understanding, everyone around him has to move through his doubt. Every night he gathers his courage and strength and attempts to stave off the leaking dark, but each time the doubt wins and the world is polluted by his failure.

49

The myth of the Birds

There are **birds** in the village, black and shiny and silent. They sit on the rooftops and high in the trees, watching down on the everyday passing by. These birds are like a Corvus, a crow or a rook or a raven, it is difficult to identify any distinguishing features as they are so often seen in silhouette, sunny day or deep in shade these birds are black as cut outs.

50

If you look through binoculars, and the sun is in the right position and the birds turn in just the right direction then you'll see that the birds have no eyes. They fly and hunt by night, using sound and a familiarity with the shapes of the buildings to navigate. During the day they map the village and its people by the noise of their footsteps, the creak of the trees, the rasp of warming brick and pink of cooling terracotta tile.

The only time you'll see them fly during the day is on Sundays when the meat is cooked outside. They circle and breathe in the sweet smoke. They have evolved as the village has and now they fit this place like they could no other, these smoking birds of the village of seven trees.

OUTSIDERS
OF THE VILLAGE

The myth of Waste

The council collects the household **waste** every two weeks here in the village, as they do with every other town and village in the county, but they move quickly through the few little streets and stay uncharacteristically quiet as they pick up the bins and bags in their crushing rushing truck.

51

They are not part of this place and they feel it, know it, so best to get it done and be gone before they have a chance to think too much or question too deeply.

They lost one of their number here, years back, no one knows his name, none of them were part of the run back then, but they heard from others who knew people who knew that team that lost one of their own.

He crossed over, they said, a villager called and the workman came, willingly. They covered for him, obviously, they told his wife that he had not been seen that day, that he often avoided work and that they assumed that he had another family in the north of the county, other commitments than her. It hurt, but it was easier than the truth.

The myth of the Cars

There is a road that winds through the village, it comes from the outside and goes back to the outside and for a few short minutes it is here, inside.

The villages West and East are proper places in their own way and those people living there are fine and decent, so they find reasons to go the longer way 'twixt one or another place.

52

Cars can drive through the village and they do so every day in their hundreds, but sometimes they cough and splutter, their electronic warning lamps flicker and their exhausts scrape as if they crouch nearer to the ground here, scuttling like chastised dogs.

You see them wheezing at the side of the street, owners peering at gauges and levels, hoping to cool them down with open bonnets and engines ticking.

They get through eventually, like driving over a high mountain pass, the air is too thin for them here, but if they keep going they soon pass on into the thicker air they are used to.

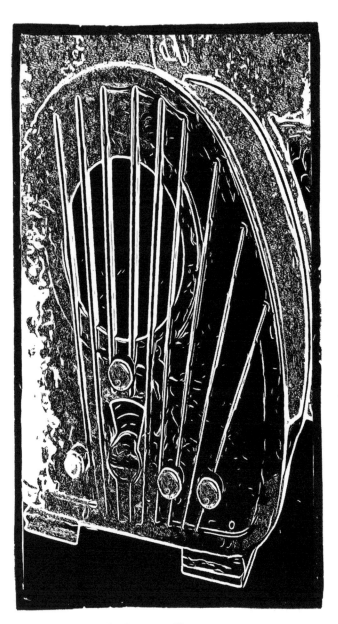

The myth of the Radio

Winchurst is a neighbouring village, you can walk there in twenty minutes if you don't drag your feet. It is not very large, certainly not large enough for a shop or a pub. There are fifteen or so houses visible from the road, but no people live here.

53

The village is maintained, gardens tended, windows cleaned, no one passing through would think it was anything other than a peacefully quiet place, silent in fact.

No one has lived in Winchurst for nearly a century. There were villagers here once, perfectly happy and honest folk, living their perfectly normal lives. As the centuries turned they moved with the times, the modern accoutrements of the twentieth century began to filter their way in common usage.

The **radio** was the real tipping point, there has not been a living resident in Winchurst since that first crackling broadcast was tuned to. That could never be countenanced, not something that could read such wavelengths. The villagers regret their actions now, they understand that times must be moved with, not fought. But is is too late to undo what was done to Winchurst.

The myth of Planes

This corner of the world is a little way away from the other places around it, but it is in no way isolated, the traffic keeps driving through, the tourists stop for their photographs and overhead, little **planes** buzz across the sky, stitching thin white lines across the blue quilt.

54

There is a little local airstrip a few miles to the north-west that has its share of pleasure flyers, the well healed commuters and day trippers, flying single engine light aircraft well below the big boys cruising overhead. When the pilots fly a little too close, a little too low, their engines can cut out, not every time and not for very long, but it happens.

No one loses control, no one crashes, the engines cough splutter and die for a few moments, there is a silence and then the pilots regain control, engines turn over and the moment has past. The villagers maintain a simple mown strip of land to the western approach to the village just in case the pilot lacks experience or the plane is poorly maintained, no one wants an accident.

On a summer's day the villagers sit and listen out for the momentary silences amidst the drone, and smile.

The myth of the Centaur

There is a big city three days walk to the north and then three days to the west, if you walk with an eye on lunch and a foot on dinner. At the very centre of this city is a man on a horse. Both man and horse are cast in metal, cast together like a **centaur** 55

These two are markers of exactitude, place makers for something that every place has but few, if any, know. These two, this one, are not just at the centre, they are the centre. The maps and signs that show a distance, to and from, all measure to this point, this mathematical heart, this pivot pin on which the city can turn.

The village also has its centre marked, not with a statue but with an iron column. The column is thin and old and you might mistake it for a sign post that has lost its sign, a lamppost that has lost its lamp. Look again and you might be able to tell that this is solid iron, pitted with age and dark with experience. The column stands up a little way out of the ground but extends deep down into the chalk, and through to the warming rock below that.

This column is the pin around which this place's particular reality turns.

Afterword

The Village of Seven Trees is real enough, it has a name which I have not mentioned here and a history which I have only begun to set out. In writing down these tales many others have had to be put aside, this is a place that gathers stories around itself like blankets on a cold night, and the nights here can get very cold indeed. Every tale told here can be traced back to a place, a person, a memory, an event or an object, they all sit comfortably together in the way this villages recollects itself. Ask a villager and they'll tell you not one of these tales are true, ask again and they'll smile a knowing smile and perhaps they will tell you a new tale, one not laid down here. You can find you own truth, if you go looking, this is place where secrets are close to the surface and one does not have to dig very far to unearth something of the 'other'.

The village is quite close, you could be there in an hour or a day or a week and when you got there you would find everything was as I have described, or a little different, depending on which eyes you bring with you. Everyone here will be waiting.

Jon A Mortimer - villager

Printed in Great Britain
by Amazon.co.uk, Ltd.,
Marston Gate.